WITH

AGAIN, JOSEFINA!

JOSEFINA · 1824

BY VALERIE TRIPP

ILLUSTRATIONS JEAN-PAUL TIBBLES

VIGNETTES SUSAN MCALILEY

THE AMERICAN GIRLS COLLECTION®

Published by Pleasant Company Publications
© Copyright 2000 by Pleasant Company

For information, address: Book Editor, Pleasant Company Publications,
8400 Fairway Place, P.O. Box 620998, Middleton, WI 53562.

Printed in Singapore.
00 01 02 03 04 05 06 07 TWP 10 9 8 7 6 5 4 3 2 1

The American Girls Collection® and logo, American Girls Short Stories™,
the American Girl logo, Josefina®, and Josefina Montoya®
are trademarks of Pleasant Company.

Edited by Camela Decaire, Nancy Holyoke, and Michelle Jones
Designed by Laura Moberly and Kimberly Strother
Art Directed by Kimberly Strother

Library of Congress Cataloging-in-Publication Data

Tripp, Valerie, 1951-
Again, Josefina! / by Valerie Tripp ;
illustrations, Jean-Paul Tibbles ; vignettes, Susan McAliley.
p. cm. — (The American girls collection)
Summary: Nine-year-old Josefina wants to give up learning to play the
piano until she sees how much joy her music gives to her baby nephew.
Discusses the importance of music on the New Mexican frontier and
describes how to dance La Vaquerita.

ISBN 1-58485-032-9
[1. Piano Fiction. 2. Music Fiction.
3. Mexican Americans Fiction. 4. New Mexico Fiction.]
I. Tibbles, Jean-Paul, ill. II. Title. III. Series.
PZ7.T7363 Ag 2000   [Fic]—dc21   99-38623 CIP

The
AMERICAN GIRLS
COLLECTION™

OTHER AMERICAN GIRLS
SHORT STORIES:

FELICITY'S DANCING SHOES

KIRSTEN AND THE NEW GIRL

ADDY'S LITTLE BROTHER

SAMANTHA SAVES THE WEDDING

MOLLY AND THE MOVIE STAR

PICTURE CREDITS
The following organizations have generously given permission to reprint
illustrations contained in "Looking Back": p. 32—Orchid Photographics, photo
by Connie Russell; p. 33—Centennial Museum, The University of Texas at El Paso;
p. 34—Private collection; p. 35—Theodore Gentilz (1819-1906), *El convite para el baile*
(Invitation to the dance), Yanaguana Society Collection, Daughters of the Republic of
Texas Library; p. 36—Jarabe Tapatío, Instituto Nacional de Asuntos Jurídicos, used
with permission (detail); p. 38—Corbis; p. 39—Palace of the Governors Collections,
Museum of New Mexico, Santa Fe.

TABLE OF CONTENTS

JOSEFINA'S FAMILY

PAPÁ
Josefina's father, who guides his family and his rancho with quiet strength.

ANA
Josefina's oldest sister, who is married and has two little boys.

JOSEFINA
A nine-year-old girl whose heart and hopes are as big as the New Mexico sky.

FRANCISCA
Josefina's fifteen-year-old sister, who is headstrong and impatient.

CLARA
Josefina's practical, sensible sister, who is twelve years old.

TÍA DOLORES
*Josefina's aunt, who
has lived far away in
Mexico City for ten years.*

ANTONIO
*Ana's youngest
little boy, who is
one year old.*

Josefina and her family speak Spanish, so you'll see some Spanish words in this book. If you can't tell what a word means from reading the story or looking at the illustrations, you can turn to the "Glossary of Spanish Words" on page 46. It will tell you what the word means and how to pronounce it.

Remember that in Spanish, "j" is pronounced like "h." That means Josefina's name is pronounced "ho-seh-FEE-nah."

AGAIN,
JOSEFINA!

Josefina slid her hand along the piano's smooth surface and admired the way the firelight was reflected in the shiny, polished wood. It was a cold evening, and Josefina and her family were gathered around the hearth in the family *sala*. Josefina was supposed to be knitting, but she couldn't resist touching the piano. It was so beautiful! Her aunt, Tía Dolores, had brought it all the way from

Mexico City when she'd come to live
with Josefina's family on their *rancho*.

Tía Dolores glanced up now and
smiled at Josefina. "You love the piano,
don't you, Josefina?" she said.

"*Sí,*" said Josefina earnestly. "I do."

Papá put down the piece of harness
he was mending and asked politely,
"Please, Dolores, won't you play for us?"

"Oh, yes, please play!" said Josefina
and her sisters Ana, Francisca, and Clara.

"Very well," said Tía Dolores. She
sat at the piano and began to play a soft,
sweet song. Josefina thought it sounded
like a lullaby that a mother might sing to
her baby. She couldn't help swaying back
and forth in time to the music. Papá and

all her sisters had dreamy, faraway looks on their faces, as if they were remembering something happy. The music seemed to have cast a spell over them.

As Josefina watched Tía Dolores's hands gracefully moving over the keys, she was filled with longing. Oh, how she wished she could make music, too!

When the song ended, Josefina burst out, "Tía Dolores, do you think I could learn to play? Would you teach me?"

Tía Dolores looked pleased. "You must ask your papá," she said. "If he gives his permission, then I'll be glad to teach you."

Josefina turned to Papá. "May I, Papá?" she asked.

"May I, Papá?" Josefina asked.

Papá thought for a moment and then answered slowly. "You have many responsibilities, Josefina," he said. "Your sister Ana depends on you to help her look after her littlest boy, Antonio. And all of us depend on you to do your chores. Can you meet your responsibilities and take piano lessons, too?"

"Sí, Papá!" said Josefina.

But Papá still did not say yes. "It's not easy to learn to play the piano," he said. "It takes time and practice and patience. And even then, not everyone has a gift the way your Tía Dolores does. Are you ready to work very hard? Because if you aren't serious, you'll waste Tía Dolores's time."

"I'll try my best," said Josefina. "I promise."

"All right, then," said Papá, smiling at her eagerness. He turned to Tía Dolores. "This is very kind of you," he said.

"Oh, it will be a pleasure!" said Tía Dolores. "I've already seen what a good student Josefina is while I've been teaching the girls to read and write."

"Sí," said Ana, the eldest sister. "Josefina's the quickest of us all. She's the best student."

Josefina bent her head to hide her pleased smile. She knew that what Ana said was true, and it made her quite proud.

"You're all good students," said Tía Dolores to the sisters. "Would any of you like to learn to play the piano, too?"

"No, thank you," said Ana sweetly. "I wouldn't like to be the center of attention the way you are when you play the piano. It would make me nervous to have so many people looking at me."

"Oh, that wouldn't bother *me!*" said Francisca. "But I don't want to learn to play, because if I'm sitting on the piano bench playing music at a party, then I can't be dancing! Where's the fun in that?"

Everyone laughed except Clara, who shook her head at Francisca's silliness. Then Clara said,

"Frankly, I don't see the purpose of learning to play the piano. Making music just isn't practical. It's not like weaving, where you have cloth to show for all your work."

"Well," said Tía Dolores, smiling at Josefina. "I guess you are my only piano student. We'll begin tomorrow morning."

Josefina smiled back. "I can't wait!" she said. She felt excited and eager and confident. Soon, *soon*, she'd be able to play enchanting music just as Tía Dolores did!

✻

"Again, Josefina," said Tía Dolores.

"Sí," said Josefina. She tried hard not
to sigh as she struggled for what seemed
like the hundredth time to play the notes
correctly. Were *all* her piano lessons going
to be as long and discouraging as this
first one? Learning to play the piano
was not at all what Josefina had expected.
It was much harder. There was so much
to remember! And Tía Dolores was so
strict!

"Keep your feet flat on the floor,"
Tía Dolores had said at the beginning of
the lesson. "Keep your back straight. Keep
your shoulders square. Keep your wrists
level with your arms. Keep your fingers
curved, as if you were holding a ball."

By now, Josefina ached all over. She slumped a little bit, and Tía Dolores tapped her back. "Up straight, Josefina," she said. "Now, try it again. Begin with the thumb of your right hand and play the notes up—*one, two, three, four, five.* And then down—*five, four, three, two, one.* Then switch to your left hand. Begin with your thumb and play the notes down—*five, four, three, two, one.* And then up—*one, two, three, four, five.*"

Josefina tried, but somehow her fingers would not do what she wanted them to do, and her left thumb hit the wrong note. Instantly, Tía Dolores said, "Start over. Remember, fingers curved. Back straight. Now, again, Josefina."

I wouldn't mind being uncomfortable, thought Josefina, *if only I were making music.* But so far, all she'd played was the same ten notes over and over again. It didn't sound like music. It sounded like water dripping into a puddle! It was not the least bit pretty. *Especially since I never do it without making a mistake,* thought

Josefina nervously. And of course the more she worried about making mistakes, the more she made. She was sure Tía Dolores must think she was terrible!

But when the lesson finally came to an end, Tía Dolores seemed cheerful enough. "Practice between lessons," she said. "That's the way to improve."

"Sí, Tía Dolores," said Josefina. She thought, *I certainly can't get any worse!*

That very afternoon, when it was time for her to take care of Ana's little boy, Antonio, Josefina put him in his cradle. Antonio looked surprised, because Josefina usually played with him. "I want you

12

to sleep now," Josefina said firmly, "so I can go practice the piano."

Josefina rocked Antonio gently and sang to him. His eyelids drooped, then closed.

Good! thought Josefina.

But the second she stopped singing, Antonio's big brown eyes popped open, and he was wide awake. "More!" he demanded.

Josefina groaned. "You're not going to fall asleep, are you?" she asked Antonio.

Antonio just smiled and reached his arms to her. "Up!" he said.

Josefina lifted him out of his cradle. She could see that Antonio was not going to let her play the piano when she was supposed to be playing with *him*.

❀

Over the next few weeks, it never got any easier to find time to practice between lessons. Lessons didn't get any easier, either. Josefina began to dread them. It seemed to her that Tía Dolores winced whenever she hit a sour note, which was often. She was sure that Tía Dolores must be tired of saying, "Again, Josefina. Try it again."

One day, Josefina hurried through her afternoon chores so that she'd have a few minutes to practice before it was time to help prepare dinner. She sat at the piano and dutifully practiced the tiresome, tuneless exercises Tía Dolores was trying to teach her. She hit lots of wrong notes, as usual.

Suddenly Josefina was aware of giggling behind her. She looked over her shoulder, and there was Francisca, pretending to dance to her playing. Francisca swooped around the room, then tripped over her own feet. She looked as clumsy as Josefina's music sounded. Clara was watching, trying to stifle her giggles.

Josefina stopped playing.

"Oh, don't stop!" teased Francisca. "I want to finish my dance."

"Sí," added Clara. "Play it again."

Usually Josefina could laugh when her sisters teased her. But right now all her frustration and disenchantment with the piano boiled over. "Stop it!" she said sharply.

"Oh, Josefina, don't be so cross," said Francisca. "We were just having fun with your music."

"The music is not fun for *me*," said Josefina grimly. "I make too many mistakes."

Clara and Francisca exchanged a glance.

"Papá warned you, Josefina," said Clara matter-of-factly. "But you wouldn't listen. You probably thought that learning to play the piano would

come as easily to you as reading and writing did." She shook her head. "Well, I think you'd better face the fact that it does not."

Josefina could not stand to hear another word—even though she knew Clara was right. With a tremendous *bang!* she slammed the lid shut over the keys.

She grabbed her shawl, ran out of the room, and did not stop running until she reached the stream.

Josefina sank down on the rocky bank and sat hidden under her shawl with her arms wrapped around her knees and her head bowed. She felt angry at the piano, angry at her sisters, angry at Tía Dolores, and, most of all, angry at herself for being such a failure.

"Josefina, child, what's the matter?" someone asked.

It was Papá.

Josefina jumped to her feet to stand politely in front of her father. "Please, Papá," she said. "I want to stop taking piano lessons."

Papá frowned. "Tía Dolores has been generous enough to spend time teaching you," he said. "It would be disrespectful of you to quit now. Why do you want to?"

Josefina answered in a small voice. "Because I'm doing so badly."

"In that case," said Papá firmly, "you'll just have to practice more."

More? Josefina's heart sank. Practicing already used up every free minute she had, and she couldn't neglect her chores! "I just don't know where I'll find the time," she said.

Papá raised his eyebrows. "Look harder," he said.

❋

Josefina could think of only one thing to do, and that was to do two things at once. She decided she'd have to start practicing at the same time that she was doing her chores.

She began the very next day.

Josefina pretended to be sitting up straight on the piano bench when she was really sitting on a stool husking corn.

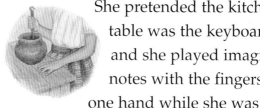

She pretended the kitchen table was the keyboard, and she played imaginary notes with the fingers of one hand while she was stirring a bowl of chiles with the other hand. She practiced curving her fingers properly while she was taking apples one by one out of the storage bin, and she kept her wrists level with her arms while she carded wool. When she went to the stream to get water for the household, she hummed the notes from her lessons over and over until they were fixed in her brain.

After a few days, her fingers worked a *little* better at lessons. Tía Dolores rewarded her by giving her a song to learn. It was only a short song with a simple tune, but it sounded very pretty when Tía Dolores played it. Josefina was pleased. At last she'd be making music! But when Josefina tried to play the song, her fingers stumbled so badly that the tune was lost in wrong notes.

One afternoon, after her lesson with Tía Dolores, Josefina had a few extra minutes before she had to take care of Antonio. She sat by herself at the piano and tried to play the simple tune Tía Dolores was teaching her. She didn't realize that anyone had come into the room until Ana tapped her on the shoulder.

"I'm sorry to interrupt your practice," said Ana. "But I need you to look after Antonio." Antonio squirmed out of Ana's arms to get to the floor. Then he began in his funny, staggering way to walk to Josefina.

Josefina held her arms out to Antonio. "I'm glad to stop playing," she said to Ana. "I'm only making mistakes anyway."

Ana smiled sympathetically.

Josefina scooped up Antonio and hugged him. She smiled a cheerless smile at Ana. "I know I'm terrible," she said. "It's embarrassing! I'd like to give up." She admitted the truth to Ana. "If I can't play well, I don't want to play at all."

"Oh," said Ana. "I hope you won't give up. I've been watching, and I've seen how you've been trying to practice while you're doing chores." She nodded at Antonio, who was busy tugging on Josefina's braid. "I don't know if my

23

fine fellow here will let you practice or
not. But give it a try." Then Ana kissed
Antonio's cheek and left.

Josefina held Antonio on her lap
and looked him in the eye. "Watch out,"
she warned him. "I'm going to practice.
It'll sound so bad it'll probably make
you cry!"

Antonio gave Josefina a happy,
drooly, baby grin as she gently put him
on the floor. He stood next to the piano
bench and slapped the top with his hand,
as if he were saying, "Begin!"

When Josefina began to play,
Antonio crowed with delight. He bounced
himself up and down on his chubby legs
in time to the music. He bounced with

*Antonio bounced himself up and down on his
chubby legs in time to the music.*

so much enthusiasm that he fell, *plop*, on his bottom.

Josefina stopped playing to help him, but he popped back up to his feet by himself and said, "Again, Josefina! Again!"

Josefina laughed out loud. "At least *someone* likes my music!" she said. Josefina was so cheered, she played the song again. She stopped worrying about making mistakes and played just for the fun of it. Pretty soon, Antonio began to dance. He'd take a few steps and fall, then get right back up, spin around, and fall again. But he never cried, and he never gave up. He kept trying to dance, even though he was really terrible at it.

He was giggling so hard he couldn't even *walk* three steps without falling.

As she watched Antonio, Josefina realized, *No one expects Antonio to walk perfectly. He's just learning. And no one expects me to play the piano perfectly, either, because I'm just learning, too.*

Josefina felt happier at the piano than she ever had before. She played her song louder and faster, again and again. She was making lots of mistakes. But Antonio didn't care, and neither did she!

Josefina was surprised when she heard someone clapping behind her. She stopped playing and turned to see Papá. He was smiling.

"Well!" said Papá. "That didn't

sound as if it were being played by someone who wanted to give up music."

Josefina smiled back at Papá. "I don't want to give it up anymore," she said.

"That's good!" said Papá. He bent down to pick up Antonio, who was pulling on his pants leg. "What made you change your mind?"

Josefina laughed. "Antonio did," she said. "I played a song that Tía Dolores taught me, and he really liked it."

"May I hear your song?" asked Papá.

"Sí!" answered Josefina with a big grin. "I'm happy to play it again."

VALERIE TRIPP

Valerie, Granger, and Suzanne Tripp

When I was Josefina's age, I had a hard time learning to play the clarinet. I made a lot of mistakes—as you can tell by my brother's expression!

Valerie Tripp has written twenty-nine books in The American Girls Collection, including eight about Josefina.

Looking Back 1824

A PEEK INTO
THE PAST

Rancho Life in 1824

A New Mexican landscape

Life was hard for New Mexican settlers like the Montoyas. It was difficult to raise crops and animals on the dry, mountainous land. Drought was a constant worry, and so were sudden floods. Lightning, mountain lions, and rattlesnakes killed farm animals, and sometimes even people. Music brought a welcome break from all the work and worry.

There was no television or radio on the New Mexican frontier, and even books were rare. Settlers counted on musicians for laughter and enter-tainment. Music often provided a reason for the people of a village to gather together and laugh and share stories. Music was a part of every celebration.

A musician playing his guitar

Settlers had many occasions to celebrate. The return of a trading caravan, the arrival of family or friends from another village, and weddings and baptisms were all cause for a *fandango*, or informal dance. On the day of a fandango, musicians rode a wagon through the countryside to announce the fandango. Some people would join the group, following along to wherever the fandango was

A woman dressed for a fandango

to be held. By evening, everyone knew where to gather for the party.

As soon as darkness fell, the dancing would begin. To start the fun, the first

Musicians announcing a fandango

dance might be the *vals de la escoba*, or "dance of the broom." The guests lined up on both sides of the room. One boy would begin dancing with a broom. When he dropped the broom, that was the signal for everyone to find a partner as fast as possible!

Another popular dance was the *vals chiquiao*, or "courting dance." When

A courting couple dancing

a couple are courting, they are getting to
know each other. During this waltz, the
musician picked out couples to play a
game. The girl was seated in a chair. Her
partner had to kneel before her and make
up a verse of poetry. If she didn't like his
verse, she wouldn't finish the dance with
him! The verses were often silly, such as:

Milk I like
And coffee too.
But more I like
To dance with you!

Music and song weren't just for celebrations. They brightened the settlers' daily chores, too. There was even a song about sweeping:

I sing while I sweep my room,
'Tis then I delight in song.
All women while they're sweeping
Sing as they wield the broom.
Forgotten are sadness and weeping,
And boredom takes his flight!

Broom

Parents also used music to teach children Spanish history and pass along their traditions, faith, and values. Many

New Mexican settlers had no opportunity to learn to read and write. Their wisdom was passed on to their children through stories, sayings, poems, and songs they knew by heart. Some songs had religious themes, and others told of Spanish kings and queens and the history of Spain. Parents also shared entertaining stories, called *cuentos*, or sayings, called *dichos*, that taught a lesson. Tía Dolores often repeated the dicho "The saints cry over lost time" to remind Josefina and her sisters to keep busy.

A Spanish king and queen

Musicians and singers usually had

no formal music train-
ing. They played simple
handmade guitars and
violins. A piano like Tía
Dolores's was rare on the New
Mexican frontier! But musicians
were highly honored by the people.
Many made their living traveling
from village to village. They sang
ballads, or long stories set to music, in
exchange for food and lodging.

Learning to play an instrument
like the guitar or piano was certainly
difficult, as Josefina found out, but being
able to bring happiness to the people
around you made all the hard work
worthwhile.

An American Girls Pastime

DANCE
LA VAQUERITA

Learn a special New Mexican dance.

Tía Dolores brought the latest songs and dances from Mexico City and taught them to Josefina and her sisters.

New Mexican dances are usually very lively. *La vaquerita* is the dance of "the little cowgirl." It is a fast, active dance, with lots of skipping and hopping. Practice this dance just as Josefina might have. Dress as she would have dressed, too, in a full skirt that will swirl as you spin around!

YOU WILL NEED:

A partner

*Dance music**

*Ask your librarian for recordings of Spanish folk music.
Look for **Spanish Folk Songs of New Mexico** and
Spanish & Mexican Folk Music of New Mexico,
cassette tapes by the Smithsonian Institution
Folkways Series.*

1. Stand beside your partner. Hold your partner's hands so that your inside arms are crossed between you, as shown.

2. Skip forward 4 skips. Then skip backward 4 skips.

3. Still holding hands, raise your arms above your heads to make a bridge.

4. Now both of you duck under the bridge and turn around.

5. Do not let go of each other's hands! You should end up holding hands in your starting position.

6. Repeat steps 2, 3, 4, and 5. As you get better at the dance, make up your own patterns of skipping and turning.

cuentos *(KWEN-tohs)*—stories or folktales

dichos *(DEE-chohs)*—proverbs or wise sayings

fandango *(fahn-DAHN-go)*—a big celebration or party that includes a lively dance

la vaquerita *(lah vah-keh-REE-tah)*—the little cowgirl

rancho *(RAHN-cho)*—a farm or ranch where crops are grown and animals are raised

sala *(SAH-lah)*—a room in a house

sí *(SEE)*—yes

tía *(TEE-ah)*—aunt

vals chiquiao *(vahls chee-kee-AH-o)*—courting dance

vals de la escoba *(vahls deh lah es-KO-bah)*—dance of the broom